W9-BEL-494

DISCARD

For all the children I have loved in my life
—V.M.

For Beth and the kids
—B.W.

Copyright © 2010 by Vicki Myron • All rights reserved. Except as permitted under the U.S. Copyright Act of 1976, no part of this publication may be reproduced, distributed, or transmitted in any form or by any means, or stored in a database or retrieval system, without the prior written permission of the publisher. • Little, Brown and Company • Hachette Book Group • 237 Park Avenue, New York, NY 10017 • Visit our website at www.lb-kids.com • Little, Brown and Company is a division of Hachette Book Group, Inc. • The Little, Brown name and logo are trademarks of Hachette Book Group, Inc. • First Edition: October 2010

Library of Congress Cataloging-in-Publication Data • Myron, Vicki. • Dewey's Christmas at the library / by Vicki Myron and Bret Witter ; illustrated by Steve James. — 1st ed. • p. cm. • Summary: After finding a red ball of yarn, Dewey the cat, who lives in the Spencer, Iowa, public library, finds a way to help decorate the Christmas tree. • ISBN 978-0-316-06872-7 • 1. Dewey (Cat)—Juvenile fiction. [1. Dewey (Cat)—Fiction. 2. Cats—Fiction. 3. Christmas—Fiction. 4. Christmas trees—Fiction. 5. Libraries—Fiction.] I. Witter, Bret. II. James, Steve, 1973– ill. III. Title. • PZ7.M9964De 2010 • [E]—dc22 • 2010001253

SC • 10 9 8 7 6 5 4 3 2 1 • Printed in China • The illustrations for this book were done in Corel Painter X. The text was set in Caxton.

Dewey's
Christmas at the Library

by Vicki Myron and Bret Witter

illustrated by Steve James

Little, Brown and Company

New York Boston

Snow and ice, twinkling lights. Kids bundled up on a cold winter night. Hot chocolate and Santa Claus and decorations just right.

In the small town of Spencer, Iowa, Christmas was everyone's favorite time of the year.

Everyone, that is, except Dewey Readmore Books,
the town's one-year-old library cat. Dewey, you see,
was just learning about holidays.

On Halloween, Dewey
discovered candy.

He slept through Thanksgiving.

So when the giant Christmas tree box came out of storage,
Dewey didn't know what to expect.

But when he saw those tree branches,
Dewey knew just what to do.
He sniffed and licked and cuddled them.
And hopped and wrestled and rolled.
I got a present, he sang as he danced.
A great big Dew-licious present.

Glitter came next. . . .

Then angels . . .

tinsel . . .

lights . . .

Dewey was having the time of his life.

And then everything went quiet.
Too quiet.
Dewey's friend, Vicki the librarian, had been helping
the children at the craft table. She looked around.
"Where's Dewey?" she wondered.

All of a sudden, Dewey came racing past.
But he didn't look like himself.
He looked like . . .
a great big marshmallow cat!

The children chased him left . . .
then right . . .
to the front . . .
and the side . . .
until they finally caught him in the picture book aisle.

"Don't worry, Dewey." The oldest boy laughed. "It's just a paper bag."

Dewey was free, but he was not happy. *Nasty bag monster*, he thought, curling up in a wreath to lick his fur.

But it was Christmastime! Excitement was in the air! Before he even finished licking his tail, something new caught Dewey's eye.

If I *sneak*, he thought, *and stretch and pounce, I think I can . . .*

Catch that skinny red mouse!

Dewey swung on the end.
The yarn bounced on his head.
He chased and reached and pounced again.
The ball tackled *him* instead.

And the next thing Dewey knew,
he was all tangled up in red yarn.

"Dewey's funny," a little girl said.
Dewey looked up. All the children were watching him.
And behind them was a big, beautifully decorated Christmas tree.
Wowzy whiskers, Dewey thought as he looked at the tree.
It's . . . it's Dew-rific.
And it's all for me!

All day, Dewey lay
happily under his tree.

That night, he explored.
Up and down, round and round,
Dewey and his red yarn wound
through the branches
and the decorations on the tree.

"Oh, my," Vicki said when she saw the tree the next morning. It was covered with yarn. And it looked . . . *fantastic*!

"Great idea, Dewey!" Vicki said. Then she smiled, petted Dewey on the head, picked up the tree, and carried it right out the front door.

Trailing behind her, like a lost kitten, was Dewey's new ball of yarn.

But . . . it's mine, Dewey thought.

That day, the library was closed. So Dewey moped. *Yuck*, he said to his food. *Double yuck*, he said to his water dish. He pushed away his favorite toy. He ignored his bed. *Christmas is lonely*, Dewey thought, *even with the wreaths and lights.*

Dewey was still curled up on the floor when
the librarians came back Monday morning.

First they brought the stuffed cats.
So what? Dewey thought.

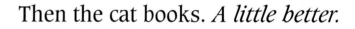

Then the cat books. *A little better.*

Then . . .

MY TREE! MY TREE!
MY DEW-RIFIC TREE!

"We won first prize," Vicki said, pointing to the blue first-place ribbon. "And it was all because of your yarn idea, Dewey."

But Dewey didn't care about first prize. He was just happy to have his Christmas tree back. And he knew, deep in his heart . . .

The award wasn't ALL because of him.
He had a *little* help.

Dewey Loves Christmas!

And now Dewey wanted to share his Dew-licious tree—and his special first Christmas—with all his friends, too.

Friends like YOU.

Jefferson Lincoln Elementary

400 W. Summa

Centralia, Washington

360 - 330 -7636

140082 EN
Dewey's Christmas at the Library

Myron, Vicki
ATOS BL 2.7
Points: 0.5

DATE DUE

MAY 17	JAN 09	
MAY 3 0	MAR 2 0	
NOV 0 6	MAY 09	
NOV 2 0		
DEC 1 2		
FEB 12		